Mitz and Fritz of Germany

Madeline Brandeis

Edition : Culturea (Hérault, 34)
Contact : infos@culturea.fr
Print in Germany by Books on Demand
Design and layout : Derek Murphy
Layout : Reedsy (https://reedsy.com/)
ISBN : 9791041849208
Légal deposit : August 2023

Mitz And Fritz Of Germany

CHAPTER I

"FOOLISH FRITZ"

Toys! Toys! Toys! All over the room—toys!

It was a big, comfortable room with a work bench in it, and shelves and a table full of paints and pots of glue.

On the window seat in a corner sat a girl, a boy, and a dog.

The girl wore a stiff white apron. Her cheeks were rosy and plump. She had a saucy look. Her big blue eyes were fixed upon the pages of a book. She was reading to the boy. The boy wore a green blouse smeared with paint. He was busily carving a wooden elephant. The dog was brown andvery long. He lay asleep beside the children with his nose on the girl's lap.

These are Mitz, Fritz, and Frank. Now you have met them. And this is their father's workshop—the workshop of a German toy maker in Nuremberg (Nū´rĕm-bûrg), city of toys.

Mitz was really Mitzi. Fritz was really Frederic. Frank, the dog, was really Frankfurter. But the former names were their nicknames.

"So! It is finished at last," said the boy who was Fritz.

He put the wooden elephant on the window sill. He stretched his arms. He was younger than his sister, and his cheeks were not so red nor was his face so saucy. He had the look of one who dreams—a happy look.

Mitzi cocked her head on one side and examined the elephant.

"It is not so bad," she said. Then she added, "For you!"

Fritz smiled. His face seemed made for smiling.

"Now, please," he said, "read some more, Mitz."

"Good. I will," answered Mitzi. "But you must carve while I read. Father will scold if he comes home and finds you idle."

Fritz began to carve a doll and Mitzi began to read. She read about Richard Wagner (Väg´nẽr), who was one of the greatest musicians that ever lived.

But suddenly she stopped reading and screamed, "Fritz! Fritz! What are you doing?"

Fritz looked down at his work and, behold, he had almost cut off the head of a doll he was carving! The poor head was hanging by a splinter.

"Shame, shame! I cannot read to you if you do such things," said Mitzi. She started to close the book.

"No, please!" begged Fritz. "I promise I will not do it again. I was thinking only of Richard Wagner. I was not looking at the doll."

"Good, then," said Mitzi, "I shall read more if you will not dream again."

But before she began to read, she got up and went to a big cupboard. From the big cupboard she helped herself to a lovely, thick slice of German brown bread. Then she took out a long knife and a long sausage, which looked very much like the long dog, Frank. She cut the sausage and put pieces of it on the bread and ate it.

"Will you have some?" she asked Fritz.

But her mouth was so full of bread and sausage that her words sounded like "Will-awamwam?"

Fritz shook his head. He was trying hard to stick the doll's head back into place. Mitzi seated herself on the window sill. She gave a piece of meat to Frank, who gobbled it up and promptly fell asleep again. Then she began to read.

"'One day,'" she read, "'when Richard Wagner was a little boy, he was watching some acrobats in the market square. A band was playing and Richard listened joyfully. They were playing a selection which he liked. It was "The Huntsman's Chorus." Little Richard—' Fritz!"

Again Mitzi screamed and put down the book in horror. The poor wooden doll had fallen to the floor. The head had rolled off. But Fritz had not noticed it at all. Fritz was reaching for a violin, which lay on a chair beside him. He was beginning to play the violin.

"This," he said, "is 'The Huntsman's Chorus.' It is what Richard Wagner heard that day and loved."

Mitzi listened. She smiled at the pretty music that Fritz made. She could not help smiling.

Often Fritz was very stupid. Often he made her very angry with his clumsy, dreamy ways and the mistakes he made. His playmates called him "Foolish Fritz." He was forever losing things and forgetting things and dropping things, making Mother sigh and Father storm.

But his music! A different thing! Mitzi thought it was the sweetest music in all the world. Even Mother, who had taught him all she knew, thought it beautiful. But Father? Ah, Father hated it. Fritz must never play when Father was around. Father was very severe, and he did not love music.

To the strains of "The Huntsman's Chorus" Mitzi nodded her head in time as she chewed on her bread and sausage. Frank awoke and gazed wonderingly at the boy with the violin. Frank was a dachshund (däks´hōōnt)—a "badger dog," in English. At one time, Frank's kind of dog was used to hunt badgers. Maybe that is why Frank seemed interested in "The Huntsman's Chorus."

Dachshunds are close to the ground, with tiny, crooked legs, and bodies that look like frankfurter sausages. Indeed, that is why Frank's real name was Frankfurter. All at once, the little dog's body bristled. He pricked up his long ears and let out a terrific bark.

Fritz stopped playing. Mitzi stopped eating. They looked up and saw what Frank had seen. The wooden elephant had disappeared from the window sill. Outside they heard a child crying.

"Give me my toy! I want my toy!" cried the child outside.

Fritz climbed upon his knees and looked out. He saw a large boy trying to take the wooden elephant away from a small boy. The younger child was crying and pulling at the toy.

"I want it! It's mine! I took it off the window!" he screamed.

But the big boy pushed so hard that the little one fell down on the sidewalk.

"It's mine," said the bully. "And don't you try to get it away again or I'll push you harder!"

Before Mitzi knew what had happened her brother had darted out of the house. Now he was standing before the big boy.

"Give that elephant to me," said Fritz. "It is mine, and you stole it."

"It's mine now," said the boy.

He smiled at Fritz's angry face and soiled workman's blouse. He stood a head taller than Fritz.

"If you want it you'll have to take it away from me," he added. He started to turn away.

Fritz jumped upon him and with both fists beat him. Fritz pounded and hit. The big boy tried to strike back, but Fritz's arms were moving like a windmill.

Mitzi stared out of the window. On her open mouth hung neglected crumbs of bread. Her eyes popped. Never had she seen her "Foolish Fritz" act like this before. He had always been so very gentle and smiling.

Frank barked. The child who had been knocked down howled. It was quite a scene. But finally Fritz ended it all by giving the big boy one mighty push. The bully fell down with a heavy thud upon the sidewalk.

Fritz snatched the wooden elephant out of the older boy's hand. He was about to go into his house when there came a terrible scream from the little boy.

"Mine! My toy! Ow!" he screamed.

Fritz stopped. He looked at the child, who was very ragged and dirty and poor. The youngster's little shoes were torn.

"Here. Take it," said Fritz, handing the elephant to the youngster. "Go home, now," he added, "before that great clumsy one snatches it away from you again."

The delighted tot ran home. The bully limped away in the opposite direction. Fritz rubbed his cheek where the fellow had struck him. Then he started to go into the house.

But as he turned, he almost ran into a great burly figure, which had planted itself in his way. It was his father!

CHAPTER II

THE TOYMAKERS

Mitzi sat upon a high stool in the kitchen, nibbling a radish. Her mother was cooking. In the workshop was Fritz being scolded by his father.

Mitzi could hear the rumbling voice of the toy maker saying, "How often must I tell you to keep your hands off that violin in working hours? If you had not been fiddling today, this never would have happened!"

There was a moment's silence, and then Mitzi again heard the angry voice: "See! I take the violin away and I hide it! Now you cannot play it ever again!"

Mitzi jumped down from her stool. She nearly stepped upon Frank, who leaped into the air with his ears waving. She burst into the workshop.

"Father!" she cried. "Wait, please!"

The toy maker was holding the violin in his hands, and there were tears in Fritz's eyes.

"I asked you to stay out of here, Mitzi," said the toy maker.

"Oh, but, Father," said the little girl, "do not take the violin away. Let me have it. I'll keep it. I'll never again allow him to play it while he is working."

But still the toy maker held the violin.

Now he turned once more to Fritz and boomed, "Do you think one makes toys to be given away to every beggar on the streets? Each time I go out, something happens. Toys are ruined or given away or stolen! And all the time you must fiddle, fiddle, fiddle!"

"Yes, yes, Father, you are right," agreed clever Mitzi. "Fritz is a stupid little donkey! But now it is Mitz who will keep the violin. You can trust me, Father. Come! Let me have the violin."

She reached up her chubby hands, and slowly a smile spread over the toy maker's red face. The toy maker had a bristly mustache that made him look like a fierce walrus. But under all his fierceness he loved his children.

"Very well," he said. "Mitzi shall keep the violin. But," he shook his finger at Fritz, "if ever I find you playing upon it again when you should be working, I shall sell it!"

At these words, Fritz looked as if the toy maker had struck him. The violin had been sent to Fritz by his mother's brother in Mittenwald, a town of violin makers. It was the little boy's dearest possession.

When their father had left the room, Fritz said, "Oh, Mitz, you are so good!"

Mitzi decided that she was hungry again, so she began digging about in the cupboard.

She said, "You are a stupid little donkey! And I am not good to you. I am not!"

"Oh, Mitz!" said her brother.

"No, I am never good to you," said Mitzi. She had found a big pickle and was beginning to gnaw at it. "And never, never will I give you the violin. Never!"

"Oh, Mitz!" said Fritz again.

"Never!" repeated Mitzi. Then she added with a smile, "Unless there is no work to be done!"

Fritz laughed.

"Come! Eat a pickle," said Mitzi.

They sat together, very happy, eating pickles. Ever since Mitzi had been a small child, she had been up to tricks and full of fun. And always, always had she been hungry!

That night when the children were in bed the toy maker and his wife talked late into the night. The toy maker was worried. He was not selling his toys.

Soon there would not be money enough in the house with which to buy food. He was telling his wife that they were very poor.

"I am tired of this life, anyway," said the toy maker. "I want to go away from Nuremberg. Here people buy only modern toys that are made by machines. In big towns people do not like the old-fashioned handmade toys."

"Where would we go?" asked his wife.

The toy maker replied, "We can wander from place to place. When towns are having fairs, all the country people come to buy. We can go from one fair to the other, selling our toys in the market squares."

"But how would we travel?" asked Mrs. Toymaker.

"Ah!" Her husband raised his finger mysteriously. "I have a secret."

Now, for a long time Mr. Toymaker had been thinking of a wandering life. He was clever with his hands and had been making a wagon, which he planned to use as a home for his family and himself on their wanderings. He told his wife about it now.

"We shall travel through Germany like gypsies," he said. "There is a saying that if you cut a gypsy in ten pieces you have not killed him. You have only made ten gypsies. Theirs is a healthful life."

Mrs. Toymaker thought the plan a good one. She usually agreed with her husband. In fact, there was only one question over which the toy maker and his wife really disagreed. That was the question of Fritz and his violin. Mrs. Toymaker thought it beautiful for people to make music. Mr. Toymaker did not. He thought it a waste of time.

He said, "One cannot touch tunes nor eat them nor play with them as one can with toys. No, Fritz shall make good, solid toys as I do, not silly, flimsy tunes, which nobody will pay to hear."

But still Mrs. Toymaker did not agree. She believed that sometimes people will pay for things, even if they cannot touch them. It was Mrs. Toymaker who had given Mitz and Fritz their books about German musicians.

It was Mrs. Toymaker who had said, "In our Germany some of the world's greatest composers of music were born. Many of them played cleverly when they were little boys. Perhaps—who knows?—my Fritz may grow to be a great musician."

But she did not say this to the stubborn toy maker.

CHAPTER III

GOODBYE TO NUREMBERG

The day before the toy maker and his family were to start on their journey, Mitz and Fritz went to the market place. They walked through the quaint old streets of Nuremberg where they had lived all their lives. Frank, the dog, followed at their heels.

They stood looking up at an ancient clock on an ancient church. Under the face of the clock sat the figure of Emperor Charles the Fifth.

When the clock struck twelve, a little door at the side opened. A row of toy knights came marching out, followed by seven electors. Each figure bowed stiffly to the Emperor as it sailed past. Then it disappeared into a door at the opposite side of the clock.

Every day this performance took place. Every day Nuremberg children gathered below to watch it. Fritz sighed when it was over.

"That is the last time we shall see it," he said.

"We shall see other things," said Mitzi. "We are going to – to – oh, to every place that we have read about!"

"We shall see the homes of great musicians," said Fritz, whose face was now beaming.

The Germans like to remember their great men. Even the school children are often taken by their teachers on trips to the towns where poets and painters and musicians lived. It is no wonder, then, that Mitz and Fritz were happy and excited about what the next day was to bring.

As they turned to leave the market place, Mitzi suddenly caught sight of some people across the street. They were walking very slowly and gazing about with the air of seeing things for the first time.

"Stay here and hold Frank," said Mitzi to her brother. "I am going over to see those strangers. I am going to ask to guide them through the church."

She crossed the street and approached the people. She felt certain that they must be Americans or English, for she had watched many like them. She decided to show how well she could speak English.

"Gute day," said Mitzi.

"Why, hello, little Gretchen!" said a jolly-looking man.

"I be Mitzi," said the little girl, with a short bow. "I will show you to the church."

The people laughed.

The jolly man said, "You wish to show us to the church? Very well. I think the church will be pleased to see us."

Mitzi took the travelers through the church. She talked a great deal, and sometimes they could not understand what she said. Nevertheless when they came out they gave her some coins. Mitzi put the coins in her pocket and bowed again.

"Danke (dän´kẽ). Danke," she said; which means "Thanks. Thanks."

The man said, "You are a good guide, and the church seemed very glad to meet us."

"Yes, ma'am," said Mitzi.

She was trying to use all the English words she knew. Then she remembered a sentence which an English boy had once taught her. He had been a very naughty boy. He had told her that it was a most polite and respectful thing to say.

So the little German girl lifted her round face to the stranger, smiled sweetly, and said, "You—are—a—silly—goose!"

Mitzi could not understand why there was a roar of laughter from her new friends. She turned and ran across the street to where Fritz and Frank were awaiting her.

"Come. We are going home to lunch now," she said to her brother.

She pulled the coins out of her pocket and showed them to Fritz. Then she pulled something else out of her pocket and began to eat. It was a bit of sausage.

They passed funny houses with pictures painted on them, and old shops full of wonderful toys and ornaments and gingerbread. They passed toy shops and sausage stands. There are a thousand different kinds of sausages in Germany.

Germany is the children's gingerbread country. Think of all the childish delights that have come out of Germany: Christmas trees, cuckoo clocks, Hansel and Gretel, Grimms' Fairy Tales, and the Pied Piper!

And toys! When a toy is marked "made in Germany," we know that it is very fine, because Germany is the toy center of the world.

In Switzerland you would climb the Alps and eat cheese. In Ireland you would kiss the Blarney Stone and eat stew. In Italy you would see the art galleries and eat spaghetti. In China you would visit the Great Wall and eat rice. But in Germany, especially if you are a child, you would go to the toy shops and eat gingerbread.

CHAPTER IV

BAYREUTH AND A PLAN

Did you ever dream of becoming so great that a whole town would exist in your memory? That is what happened in the case of Richard Wagner, the little boy who stood in a market square and listened to "The Huntsman's Chorus."

Mitz and Fritz and their parents arrived in Bayreuth (Bī´roit´) in time for the Wagner festival. People had come from all over the world to hear the great Wagner operas. They are performed in a beautiful theater built especially for that purpose.

During the festival, the whole town talks and thinks and remembers Richard Wagner. In every shop window are pictures of the composer. Even a newspaper is published which prints only matters concerning Richard Wagner.

Mitz and Fritz left their wagon home and began to wander through the woodland town. Fritz was so happy and excited that one would have thought it his own festival. He had read and heard much about Bayreuth.

Mitzi, too, was impressed. But this did not stop her from nibbling at a bar of chocolate and smearing her round face.

"What do all the blue and white banners mean?" asked Fritz.

"They are the colors of Bavaria," said Mitzi.

Just as we have our states, so has Germany hers. In each part of the country the people are different from those of other parts.

In the United States the southern people are different from the western cowboy. In Great Britain the Scotch are different from the Welsh. In Switzerland the Italian-Swiss are different from the French-Swiss.

In Germany the Bavarian is a jolly farmer The German who lives by the Rhine is fun- loving and cheerful. But the Prussian is strict and very serious.

Mr. Toymaker was a Prussian. So is the former Kaiser, who ruled Germany before the World War. Now the ex-Kaiser is living quietly in Holland, and Germany is a republic like our country.

But let us go back to Mitz and Fritz. It seems that I cannot resist telling you a few things about their country as we go along. However, I am sure Mitz and Fritz would not object to that. For all Germans want to learn, even while they play.

Mr. Toymaker tried to sell his toys in the crowded market place of Bayreuth. But he was not very successful. People were thinking only of the glorious music they had come to hear.

Visitors wandered about the town. They stood beside the grave of Wagner in the garden of his home. In this grave the musician is buried with his faithful dog.

It is here that we find Mitz and Fritz and Mrs. Toymaker. Frank lay at their feet.

"Father is so disappointed," said Mrs. Toymaker. "He has sold so few toys."

"Perhaps in the next town he will sell more," said Fritz. Then he took his mother's hand. "Please," he added wistfully, "tell us something about Richard Wagner."

Mrs. Toymaker was much like Fritz and not very much like Mr. Toymaker. Somehow she forgot her worries about not selling toys when she thought of Wagner. So she smiled and told the children this story:

"When Richard was about fourteen he went to school in Dresden. But he soon became very homesick for his family, who were living in Prague (Präk). He had no money, so he and a schoolmate decided to walk to Prague.

"It was a long distance, and the boys grew very weary and hungry. At last Richard made up his mind to hail the first coach and to beg for money. The other boy was timid and hid in the bushes.

"Richard stood in the center of the road as a coach came along. He held up his hand and the coach stopped. But the poor boy's knees were shaking, and he could hardly speak."

Mitzi interrupted her mother. "Why not?" she asked. "I would have spoken. I would have said, 'Give me money. I am hungry.'"

"Yes," laughed Mrs. Toymaker. "I have no doubt of that. For you are always hungry and you can always talk! But, you see, Richard was different."

"A bit foolish, like Fritz," said Mitzi knowingly.

The mother paid no attention to this remark but went on with her story: "The people in the coach were kind and threw money to Richard. He and his friend had a good dinner and finally reached Prague. But they say that he never forgot this experience."

A light began to shine in Mitzi's eyes as her mother finished the tale. An idea had been born in her busy little head. That evening after supper she took Fritz by the hand.

"Come," she whispered. "I have something to tell you—something very exciting." She led him away from their wagon, out upon the moonlit road. "Fritz," she said, "I have thought of a way to help Father. I thought of it after Mother told that story about Richard Wagner. Now, if Richard had been a boy musician like you, he might have played for people and—"

"Do you mean that he might have played on his trip to Prague?" asked Fritz.

"Yes," said Mitzi. "In every town. The people would have thrown him so much money that he could have bought all the bread and sausage and—"

Fritz laughed at Mitzi's wide eyes.

"Well, but what has that to do with our helping Father?" he asked.

"Don't you see?" she replied. "You shall play on the streets, and people will throw coins. Then, even if Father cannot sell toys, we shall still have money with which to buy food."

"Oh, Mitz!" said Fritz.

"Oh, whist!" cried Mitzi impatiently. "I am going to make you do it! You'll see how easy it will be."

"But Father will not let me do it," said Fritz. "He does not like my fiddling. He would punish me."

"We won't tell him," said Mitzi. "He only forbade you to play when he puts you to work. Other times, it is not wrong for you to do it. So, when Father is selling toys in the next market place, we'll run off. You shall play your violin, and pretty soon crowds of people will gather and— "

"Oh, Mi— " began Fritz.

"Oh, fiddlesticks!" snapped Mitzi. She took him firmly by the arm. "Come," she said. "It is all settled. It is a fine plan. So now let us find something to eat and then go to bed."

CHAPTER V

ALONG THE ROAD

Mr. Toymaker heard of a fair to be held in Mainz (Mīnts). So he decided to go there at once, although it was some distance from Bayreuth.

On the journey the children were kept busy. Fritz had to help his father with many things. Mitzi had to help her mother. They found no time to try their plan. But they did not forget it.

Along the road they saw much of interest. They passed small hotels for young travelers hiking about the country. In different lands there are different sports. Spain has her bullfights. England has her cricket. Switzerland's high mountains are popular for snow and ice sports. The United States plays baseball. But Germany hikes.

All over the land, in the summer time and even in winter, one meets groups of walkers. Children walk with teachers. Older children walk alone. As they walk they sing. They admire their country and learn. They stop overnight in these little youth inns—hotels made especially for boys and girls.

"Some day I am going with a group," said Mitzi. "I am going on hiking trips."

"Not until you are a bachfisch (bäk´fish)," said Fritz.

In Germany a young girl is called a "bachfisch," which means "baked fish."

But not so long ago in Germany girls did not hike and swim and play tennis. But now it is different. Girls are interested in everything, just as they are in America.

The Toymaker family journeyed through Hanau (Hä´nou), home of the Grimm brothers. The children spoke of these two devoted men, who had always worked together. Some of their stories have become famous, as, for instance, "Hansel and Gretel" and "Tom Thumb."

The family moved on toward Frankfurt.

The five Rothschild brothers had lived in Frankfurt. They had become the richest men in Europe and were called "The Five Frankfurters." Mrs. Toymaker remembered that the great poet, Goethe, had been born there.

Mitzi hoped to eat her fill of sausages. Frankfurt is supposed to be the home of the "hot dog." But she had more important hopes than eating "hot dogs." She was going to carry out her plan for Fritz's concert when they reached Mainz.

CHAPTER VI

MAINZ AND A BEGGAR

"Come quickly, Fritz. Now, we can slip away!" said Mitzi.

They were in the market place of Mainz. Their father was sitting at a booth under a striped umbrella. He was selling a few toys, and he looked more cheerful than usual.

Mitzi led her brother down the street.

"Quickly, come! We shall stand here before this big church," she said.

They had stopped in front of a beautiful old cathedral. Near by stood the statue of a man holding a sheet of paper in his hands.

"That is the statue of Gutenberg (Goo̅´tĕn-bĕrk), the inventor of printing," said Mitzi.

Fritz could not help thinking, just then, of all the great men who have come out of Germany. There was this Gutenberg, born here in Mainz. There was Professor Einstein (Īn´stīn), the famous scientist, born in Ulm. There was—

"Fritz! Fritz!" His sister was stamping her foot and screaming until she was almost purple in the face. "Will you listen?" she cried. "What are you thinking of? Come now! Stop dreaming and play your violin!"

Fritz had to laugh at her stern round face and her sharp command.

He saluted and said, "Yes, yes, General! I obey."

Then he took up his violin and began to play. Several people stopped to listen. They smiled but passed on. Mitzi stood on one foot and then on the other. Frank lay at her feet, wondering why they did not go on to explore this strange new city. Fritz played and Mitz stood, and only a few people seemed to notice them. Among these was a gentleman who put his hand into his pocket.

"Catch!" he said to Mitzi, as he threw her a coin.

After some time, Fritz grew tired and Mitzi discouraged.

"Let us go and buy sausage with this coin," said Mitzi.

She was not altogether pleased with the way things had worked out. But, anyway, she wanted to surprise her father with the small bit they had been able to make.

They turned to leave, when all at once they heard a whining sound behind them. They looked around. Sitting upon the church steps was a beggar. He wore ragged clothes and was a very old man. He held out his hand to Mitz and Fritz.

He said, "I am a beggar and I am hungry. Will you give me your coin?"

He looked miserable. Mitzi felt sorry for him. But still she thought of her father's pleasure if she should return home with sausages.

She thought how she would say to her father, "It was Fritz's music that did it."

But Fritz was tugging at her sleeve.

"Give it to him," said the boy. "See! He is very old."

Mitzi put her hand into the pocket of her little apron and pulled out the precious coin. She looked at it lovingly, then she threw it to the old man.

"Come along, Fritz," she said.

The children turned away and left a happy beggar behind.

CHAPTER VII

DOWN THE RHINE AND TROUBLES

Mr. Toymaker felt almost jolly. He counted the money he had made and chuckled.

"At last our luck has changed," he said. "I have really sold some toys. Now, let us go on. Let us wander down the Rhine and stop at friendly fairs along the way."

Mitzi was not so pleased with her day.

"Still we shall not give up," she said to Fritz. "At the next large town you must give another concert. Only we shall take care this time that there are no beggars about!"

The family left Mainz and started along the shore of the most famous river in all the world. England has her river Thames (Tĕmz). France is proud of the Seine (Sān). Italy loves the Tiber. Russia sings of the Volga. In Austria it is the Danube. But the River Rhine is dear to Germany.

Castles on every hill have ancient legends. The Toymaker family gazed upon beautiful, vine-covered hillsides and villages where people live by the making of wine. The Rhine land is a wine land. Some of the best wines in the world come from here.

Mitz and Fritz thought of the stories of Siegfried (Sēg´frēd), that great hero of Wagner's operas, "Siegfried" and "The Twilight of the Gods." In the Rhine land Siegfried was born.

They thought of Charlemagne (Shär´le-mān), that mighty conqueror, who lies sleeping in this land. They thought of dragons, of buried treasure, of brave heroes, of secret caves. The Rhine country is full of such thoughts.

Then they came to Bingen (Bĭng´ĕn).

"The Mouse Tower!" cried Mitzi.

"Tell us the story, please, Mother!" said Fritz.

The children had heard this tale many times. But never before had they heard it told while they were looking at the old tower. It stood in the center of the river.

"Long ago," began Mrs. Toymaker, "there lived a cruel bishop. When the poor people were starving, he bought all the grain in the land.

He locked it up in his barn. The hungry villagers came to steal the grain. While they were in the barn, the bishop set fire to it.

"He said, 'These people deserve to die. They are like mice stealing from a granary.'

"But soon he was punished for his wickedness. One day thousands of mice broke into his tower and ate him up. That is why this is called the Mouse Tower."

Said Fritz, "He deserved to be eaten!"

Said Mitz, "I wonder how a bishop would taste to a rat."

"Mitz! Mitz!" laughed Mrs. Toymaker. "What strange ideas you have!"

Yet Mrs. Toymaker could hardly guess what strange things Mitzi was really going to do. Even Fritz did not know. Indeed, Mitzi herself was unaware of all that lay before her.

The Toymakers traveled along the Rhine.

They passed the beautiful rock of the Lorelei and Mrs. Toymaker told Mitz and Fritz the famous legend of the beautiful maiden who sat upon the rock combing her golden hair. She sang and called to passing ships, and her voice was so beautiful that fishermen and sailors tried to reach the rock but they were always dashed to pieces on the reefs at the foot of the cliffs.

Mitz and Fritz loved this story.

The Toymakers stopped at one or two small towns. But Mr. Toymaker sold no toys. Again he grew worried. They passed happy people bathing in the river. Gay bath-houses dot the shores. Bathers bake themselves in the sun and rest beside the river.

"There is never any rest for me," sighed poor Mr. Toymaker.

"Perhaps, when we reach Coblenz (kō´blĕnts), you will sell more toys," said his wife.

"When we reach Coblenz," murmured Mitzi to Fritz, "you are to give another concert."

When they arrived in Coblenz, Mitzi said, "Come along, now, Fritz. This is our chance."

A short time later, Mr. Toymaker looked about and could not find Fritz and Mitzi.

"Where are the children?" he asked. "They are always running off."

"They have gone to the town," answered Mrs. Toymaker.

"I did not tell them they could go," said Mr. Toymaker. "What are they up to? They should stay and help me with my work."

"But they finished their work," said Mrs. Toymaker.

Mr. Toymaker grunted. He would surely have grunted more angrily had he seen what his children were doing at that moment. Fritz was standing in a far corner of the market square, playing his violin. Mitzi was standing by his side.

Coblenz is a city of manufacturing and similar industries. The fortress across the river was occupied by American soldiers after the World War. Sometimes in a quiet city people are not much hurried. Therefore they give heed to pleasant sounds. Coblenz has been a quiet city since the soldiers left.

Mitzi eagerly watched the passers-by. She smiled as Fritz played. The little dog Frank wagged his tail happily. Then he fell asleep on the sidewalk.

Soon a large number of people gathered. They stood listening.

One said to another, "The boy plays well. He is a real musician."

Several coins were thrown.

"I am right!" thought Mitzi. Her heart pounded with delight. "People will pay to hear my Fritz's music. They will!"

When the day was almost done, Fritz stopped playing. Mitzi showed him the money they had made.

"See," she said. "Enough coins to make even Father smile! Come. Let us give them to Father. How pleased he will be!"

"Now, perhaps, he will like my playing," said Fritz.

They hurried toward their wagon, where they found Mr. Toymaker very much annoyed.

"Why did you run away and not tell me where you were going?" he demanded.

Mitzi held out the money.

"See, Father," she said. "See what Fritz's music has brought!"

Mr. Toymaker looked at the coins in Mitzi's hand. Then he looked at the happy face of the little girl. And then he turned to Fritz, who was smiling at him.

"You are a very naughty boy!" he said.

The smile left Fritz's face. Mitzi caught her father's arm.

"But, Father," she said. "You don't understand. Fritz did nothing wrong. He only played his violin when he had finished the work you gave him. He played in the town, and people threw coins because they liked his music."

"What?" cried Mr. Toymaker. "Do you tell me that people paid to hear a boy scratching upon a fiddle? It is not true! Fritz has stolen this money!"

"Father!" gasped Fritz.

His face had gone white. Mitzi's eyes became two round bowls.

"Oh, Father, no!" she cried. "Fritz would never steal, and neither would I!"

"Do not say another word," commanded Mr. Toymaker. "You cannot make me believe this story. A boy's fiddling cannot more money than I can make in a week selling toys. No, you have stolen. And I will not have it."

Mrs. Toymaker tried to make him believe Mitz and Fritz. But Mr. Toymaker was very stubborn.

"They are naughty children," he said to his wife. "Mitzi is always doing things she should not do. It was she who put the boy up to it. They must be made to obey! Tonight they shall go to bed without any supper."

Fritz cried himself to sleep that night. Mitzi tried to comfort him. To be accused of stealing! That was worse than having to go to bed without supper.

"We'll show Father, Fritz," Mitzi said bravely. "You'll see."

Still her heart was heavy.

"He will never believe me," said Fritz. "If only he would let me play for him! And now he thinks that I am a thief!"

Poor, honest little Fritz!

CHAPTER VIII

BONN AND BEETHOVEN

"Please, Fritz, do not look so sad," pleaded Mitzi.

They had arrived near the town of Bonn (Bŏn) on the Rhine. In the distance they could see the buildings of a large university.

Fritz had not smiled since their terrible experience in Coblenz. Now, however, Mitzi hoped to cheer him.

"See, Fritz," she said. "We are in the town of Beethoven (Bā´tō-vĕn)."

At the sound of this name Fritz's eyes brightened. Beethoven was one of the greatest musicians that ever lived.

"I have asked Father to let us wander through the streets," said Mitzi. "We may even go to the house where Beethoven was born. Come, Fritz."

The boy and girl started off together for the pretty little village.

Later, Mr. and Mrs. Toymaker set off for the market place to sell their wares.

"I do wish you would listen to Fritz's playing," said Mrs. Toymaker, as they walked along. "He has been so unhappy since that day you scolded him. Perhaps, after all, our son may be a real musician."

"Say no more about that," growled Mr. Toymaker. "I'll have no idle musicians in my family. Look at all the starving tune makers in the world! They cannot even support themselves. No! Music is foolish!"

"But," said Mrs. Toymaker, "you forget that Beethoven— "

"He was different!" snapped Mr. Toymaker. "We cannot all be geniuses!"

So what could poor Mrs. Toymaker say? Often the good lady had wondered why it was that her husband wanted Fritz to make toys. Surely the making of toys had not proved a happy trade for Mr. Toymaker! But it was very difficult to argue with him, so his wife did not try.

The children visited Beethoven's house. It is now a museum. In it are such relics as the musician's letters, his piano, and even his ear trumpets. For Beethoven became deaf. Imagine such a thing as a deaf composer! Yet this wonderful man composed some of his most beautiful music even after he could not hear.

"I have read many things about Beethoven," said Fritz to Mitzi. "But the part I like to read about is when he was a boy."

Then Fritz told his sister some of the things he had read: "One night when Ludwig was asleep, his father came home and woke him up. He stood at this very gate and called, 'Up, up, Ludwig, and play!' His father kept him at the piano all night long. Next day Ludwig was so tired that he could not keep awake at school."

"Why did his father do that?" asked Mitzi indignantly.

"Because," answered Fritz, "he wanted Ludwig to be a great pianist and give concerts."

There is a statue of Beethoven in the main square of Bonn. In Germany a statue is called a "denkmal," which means a "think over." As Mitz and Fritz looked upon this "think over," they thought over many things.

"It seems strange," sighed Mitzi, "that Ludwig's father forced him to play, while your father forbids you to."

Fritz laughed.

"You silly!" he said. "I am not Ludwig van Beethoven."

Mitzi began to look like a fierce young lion. She really could look that way sometimes.

"No," she said, "but you are Fritz! And you can play the violin more beautifully than any other boy in the world."

"Oh, Mitz, what are you saying?" laughed her brother.

But Mitzi was firm.

"One day we shall see," she said.

Mr. Toymaker sold enough toys that day to buy dinner. Next day the family started off again along the Rhine.

Then, after many long days of traveling, the Toymakers at last reached the town of Hamelin. This is the scene of the Pied Piper tale. It is where something remarkable is supposed to have happened to children years and years ago. Hamelin is also the place where something really did happen to Mitzi.

CHAPTER IX

MITZI IN HAMELIN

Mitz was not Mitz today. She was the Pied Piper of Hamelin! She had started off for a walk through the town. With her was Frank, the long dog, and an equally long sausage. She had asked her mother's permission to go.

Mrs. Toymaker had said, "Yes, you may go. But be sure to come home early."

Fritz stayed with his father, helping him to paint some toys and to repair others. They were getting ready for a fair in Hanover, a city not far away.

So Mitzi wandered off alone—Mitz, Frank, and the sausage! They passed through an old gateway into Hamelin. What a storybook town it was! Every crooked house, every narrow street reminded Mitzi of the Pied Piper legend.

She could almost see the funny, tall man playing on his pipes. She could imagine the rats scampering after him. She could hear the voices of the children as they followed his music. For, when the Piper had charmed the terrible rats out of Hamelin, the people refused to pay him what they had promised. So the tall stranger piped the children away, in order to punish the ungrateful villagers.

Robert Browning has written a poem about it.

Hamelin is a quiet little town. Mitzi came upon an old fountain named after the rat catcher. She saw an inn called the Rat Jug. Altogether it was too magical and story-like to be true. So Mitzi became the Pied Piper.

She began to lift her feet up high. She straightened out her plump little shoulders. Then she raised the sausage to her lips. But she did not eat it. The sausage became her pipe. Marching along with Frank at her heels, she piped upon her sausage and lived the old story. A few people looked at her and smiled.

Through a narrow lane she went. It was the same lane through which the Piper had led the children. Even today it is unlawful to play a pipe in this lane. But Mitzi's pipe could only be heard by Mitzi herself. She followed the pathway out of town and upon a country road.

The lines of the poem came to her mind:

"And to Koppelberg Hill his steps addressed,And after him the children pressed."

She led her make-believe children up the mountain side—a long line of children, but really, only a long dog! They reached a cave in the hillside. The sun beat down upon them and the little dog's tongue swept the ground. This was not strange, since Frank was so close to the ground, anyway.

Mitzi sat down upon a rock and began to eat her pipe. She was still in a land of other things. She could still see the mass of children flocking after the sweet music. She could hear their laughter as they tumbled into the cave.

And then it happened! Real music! It was coming closer. A tall figure appeared over the hill.

"His queer long coat from heel to headWas half of yellow and half of red,And he himself was tall and thin,With sharp blue eyes, each like a pin."

He stood before Mitzi and stopped playing on his pipe.

He said, "Why are you not in the cave, Mitzi? Go into the cave with the other children."

"I must go home to Mother and Father and Fritz," said Mitzi. "It grows late. See! The sun is sinking."

Indeed, it had become darker, and there was a chill in the air.

"Go into the cave, Mitzi," repeated the tall stranger quietly.

Then he began to play the sweetest music that Mitzi had ever heard. He walked into the cave, prancing as he walked. Mitzi got up. She wanted to run home, but she could not. She could only follow the Piper into the cave.

Now, at the toy maker's wagon the family began to worry. It was almost dark, and Mitzi had not come home.

"I will go and find her," said Fritz.

Mrs. Toymaker decided to go along with Fritz.

Meanwhile, Mitzi was inside the cave. There she sat with many wide-eyed children. She wanted to go home. But the Piper was playing and making her happy. She felt all snuggly and contented.

Suddenly she thought of Fritz. Oh, she must go! She and Fritz had much to do. She could not stay here any longer. In the morning they were going to leave Hamelin. If she did not return to the wagon, they would go on without her.

"Let me out! Let me out!" cried Mitzi. "I must go to Fritz. Let me out!"

The Piper tried to hold her. She struggled. She kicked. She screamed.

"Stop! Stop! You are hurting me," said the Piper.

"I mean to hurt you!" she cried. "I want to go. I want Fritz."

"Then wake up, you silly," said the Piper. "For I am Fritz!"

She stopped kicking and looked. Yes, the Piper had the face of Fritz. He was Fritz! She rubbed her eyes. How could Fritz be a Pied Piper? Where did he get the cloak? She rubbed her eyes again. This time, when she looked, the Piper was not there any more, but only Fritz and her mother, laughing at her.

"Come home, you little sleepyhead," said Mrs. Toymaker, putting her arm about her little daughter.

On the way home Mitzi could not speak. And when Mitzi could not speak, there was something quite wrong or strange or exciting. This time it was something exciting. For her dream had given her a wonderful idea.

CHAPTER X

STRÖBECK AND DISGRACE

The family were wandering through the Harz (Härts) Mountains. Mitz and Fritz had never before seen so many trees nor heard such lovely bird songs. Mrs. Toymaker told them about the famous canary birds raised in the Harz Mountains.

"They are considered the finest singers in the world," she said.

The children loved to pass through tiny villages and see the quaint costumes of the peasants. In large cities the people do not wear costumes. But in mountain hamlets they often wear the dress of their ancestors.

Mitzi was much interested in costumes just now. For Mitzi was making one. She had decided to dress her brother as the Pied Piper. She was collecting every bit of red and yellow goods she could find. She was sewing, sewing, sewing as they drove along. Some of her red scraps were pink, it must be admitted. Some of her yellow scraps were white. But this did not bother Mitzi.

She was making a Pied Piper cloak for Fritz. She picked up bits of cloth along the way and washed them carefully. She begged and obtained all the rags her mother had. At the tiny windows of their wagon hung yellow curtains. Mitzi longed to use them for her precious cloak.

But when she asked for them, Mrs. Toymaker said, "If you will not tell me what you are doing, surely I cannot let you have them."

But Mitzi would not tell. It was to be a secret between Fritz and herself. When they reached the next large town, Fritz was to put on the cloak. He was to play his violin dressed as the Pied Piper. Mitzi planned to bring Mr. Toymaker to the scene of the concert. She hoped to show him at last that Fritz's music could please people and make them throw money.

Mr. Toymaker was silent and sad. He wondered what would happen to them all if his business did not improve. A gypsy life was not very pleasant, after all. A cosy home was better for a German family.

In September there was to be an important fair in the city of Leipzig (Līp´sĭk). Mr. Toymaker determined to be there. But until then they would be obliged to wander.

One day they approached the town of Ströbeck.

"Ah," said Mr. Toymaker, "we are in time for the great chess festival. People who are interested in chess come to this festival from far and near. Let us stop."

Mitzi, who was busily sewing, looked up.

"What is chess?" she asked. "Is it like cheese? Is it good to eat?"

Mrs. Toymaker laughed, "No, no, little hungry one! It is a game played on a board like checkers. This town is the only one in the world where children learn chess in school."

"In school?" asked Fritz.

"Yes," said Mrs. Toymaker. "During certain months each child goes to school with his chessboard. Children learn the old game just as you learn arithmetic."

"I think I would like that better than arithmetic," said Fritz.

"But it is a difficult game," said Mrs. Toymaker.

They made their camp near the peaceful town of Ströbeck. They noticed some peasant girls tending geese in a field.

"See, Mother," said Mitzi. "They play chess while they watch the geese."

"During the World War," said Mrs. Toymaker, "the Ströbeck money was printed with colored chessboards and chessmen upon it."

Later, the family made their way to the public square. The children enjoyed the parade of strangely dressed people. There were kings, queens, bishops and knights marching along. They represented the chessmen with which the game is played. The whole town was in a very gay mood.

Mr. Toymaker sold enough toys to cheer him somewhat. After supper they sat outside their wagon, and Mrs. Toymaker told them all she knew about this strange place.

"Chess is an ancient game," she said. "Ströbeck has been playing it for many years. Children begin to learn it when they are still babies. There once lived a boy of seven who became a champion. He even beat the village schoolmaster."

Fritz liked to hear these stories. He listened eagerly. But Mitz had only one thought these days. That thought was the costume for Fritz.

She had her eye upon the yellow curtains of the wagon. How fine they would be for her purpose! The family traveled further, and all the time Mitzi sewed. Slowly the costume grew, but too slowly for Mitzi.

One day when Mrs. Toymaker returned from the market place, she thought surely her eyes were playing her tricks. The windows of their wagon looked crooked. Then out came Mitzi. And what had happened to Mitzi? She looked crooked, too!

"Mitz, what have you done to the curtains?" asked Mrs. Toymaker.

Before Mitzi could reply, Mrs. Toymaker understood why Mitzi looked crooked. Her little red skirt was hanging in a strange, uneven way. Mrs. Toymaker inspected the curtains.

"Mitzi!" she said sternly. "You have cut pieces off the top of the curtains and tried to sew them together again."

Mitzi said nothing, but her face was flushed.

"Oh, Mitz!" continued Mrs. Toymaker. "You have cut pieces off your red skirt and tried to sew it together, too. Now it is hanging all wrong. You naughty little girl!"

Fritz was out gathering wood for the fire. Mitzi had worked alone and quickly.

"I do not know what you are up to, Mitzi," said her mother. "But you must be punished for this."

So for three days Mitzi was made to stay in the wagon alone. She could not go with the family to market. She had to eat her meals alone. She had to eat black bread and drink water like a prisoner. This was very hard for sausage-loving Mitz. She was in disgrace.

However, she bore her punishment like a man. She knew that she had done wrong. She helped her mother to arrange the curtains and to fix her skirt. She said nothing. But all the time she knew that soon the brightly colored little cloak would be finished.

CHAPTER XI

EISENACH AND BACH

"Our great chance will come in Leipzig," said Mitzi.

She was sitting on the steps of their wagon, sewing. Fritz sat beside her. He held an open book in his hands.

The Toymakers had made their camp outside of Eisenach (Ī´zĕn-äk). Mr. and Mrs. Toymaker had gone to town, leaving Mitz and Fritz with the wagon. Mitzi wanted to finish that costume before they arrived in Leipzig. Fritz was reading about Johann Sebastian Bach (Bäk), who was born in Eisenach.

"Bach came from a family of musicians," read Fritz. "The name 'Bach' means 'brook.' Beethoven once said, 'He is not a brook but an ocean!'"

"Come," interrupted Mitzi. "Try on the cloak. I am afraid I have made it too large."

"No," said Fritz, as he tried it on. "It fits me perfectly. How pretty it is, and how clever is my Mitz!"

Mitzi waggled her head proudly.

She said, "Many people will be in Leipzig for the fair. When you give your concert, I'll fetch Father and bring him to where you are playing. Oh, how surprised and pleased he'll be!"

Fritz smiled. Then he went on reading from his book while Mitzi sewed.

"'When Bach was a boy,'" read Fritz, "'his father died and he lived with his brother Christoph. One day Christoph brought home a book full of beautiful music. The little boy longed to play it. But Christoph was jealous of Sebastian's talent. He refused to let him have the music book and locked it up.

"'Poor Sebastian wanted very much to play that music. So every night he got up and stole downstairs into the music room. He pulled the book out from between the bars of the bookcase. He sat in the light of the moon and copied the notes.

"'At last, after many weeks, he had copied the whole volume. He went to sleep with his work under his pillow. He was very happy. But next day a terrible thing occurred. While Sebastian was playing the music on the harpsichord, his brother Christoph came in. When Christoph saw what the boy had done, he took away Sebastian's precious copy book.'"

"And what happened then?" asked Mitzi.

She was interested in this poor little fellow who had longed so much for music. She was very angry with the brother.

Fritz read on: "'Sebastian fell ill. He was so unhappy that he could not eat. Then, one day he discovered that he could play the beautiful music without notes. It was all written in his heart!'"

"Ah," said Mitzi. "That is good!"

"'But just as he was playing it,'" continued Fritz, "'in came his brother Christoph again— '"

"The goose!" sniffed Mitzi.

"'Christoph stood in the doorway listening,'" read Fritz. "'At first he was ready to stop the playing. But at last it dawned upon him that his little brother was truly a great artist.'"

"So he stopped being jealous?" asked Mitzi.

"Yes," said Fritz. He closed the book and sighed, adding, "It must have been terrible for Sebastian when his brother took away the music he loved."

Mitzi sighed, too. Then she jumped up quickly, frightening Fritz so that he fell off the steps.

"But now I am hungry," said Mitzi. "Let us go and get some cheese!"

CHAPTER XII

A CASTLE AND THE POET CITY

As the Toymaker family drove away from Eisenach, they passed below the Wartburg (Värt´bo͝ork) Castle. Mrs. Toymaker asked her husband to stop. She wanted the children to see this historic place. The castle stands high on a crag.

As they walked toward it, Mrs. Toymaker said, "It was here that Martin Luther translated the Bible from Latin into German so the German people could read it. There is a tale of how the Devil appeared before Luther, who threw an inkwell at the Devil's head. The spot where that inkwell hit the wall is still to be seen in the castle."

"Please tell us another story about the castle," said Fritz.

"St. Elizabeth was Countess of Wartburg," said Mrs. Toymaker. "She had a heartless husband, who did not want her to be kind to the poor and sick. Upon one occasion he met her going out of the castle carrying a basket.

"'Where are you going? And what have you in that basket?' he asked.

"Now, Elizabeth had loaves of bread in the basket. She was taking them to a poor old woman. But she was afraid of her husband's wrath.

"So she answered, 'I have only roses in the basket.'

"The Count, her husband, looked into the basket to be sure. And, behold, the Countess had spoken truthfully. The loaves of bread had been turned into roses!"

Had Mrs. Toymaker and the children gone into the castle, they would have seen pictures of this story drawn upon the walls. But they did not go inside. They went back to their wagon and proceeded on their way.

"I hope that my friend, Mr. Krauss, will be in Leipzig," said Mr. Toymaker. "Mr. Krauss is a bookseller. He will surely help me. He may even start a toy shop for me in Leipzig. I hope I shall find Mr. Krauss!"

However, before they reached Leipzig, they stopped in Weimar (Vī´mär), the "poet city."

Weimar is where Goethe (Gû´tẽ), Germany's greatest poet, once lived. School children were taught to salute the poet Goethe, when they passed him on the street. Today children are still taken to Weimar by their teachers and told about Goethe's life.

Long ago, a little boy was brought to Weimar to visit at the old poet's home. This little boy was about the same age as Fritz and also loved music. Felix Mendelssohn (Měn´děl-sōn) was his name. Goethe met young Mendelssohn in the garden and led him into the house and to the piano.

He said, "Now, make a little noise for me."

Felix played so beautifully that Goethe said, "You have given me great pleasure. What would you like me to do for you?"

Felix answered, "I should like you to kiss me."

Mitz and Fritz had heard many stories about Felix Mendelssohn. He was their mother's favorite composer.

She had told them how this wonderful boy had written music when he was only a baby. She had told them about the way Felix used to lead a big orchestra. He had been so small that he had had to stand upon a chair.

But Mrs. Toymaker did not know that her own little boy had a gift, too. Sometimes she wondered, of course. Still she agreed with Mr. Toymaker that very few people are born with genius. Only naughty little Mitz was sure because she loved Fritz so much. She loved him and made up her mind that everyone in the world was going to find out about his beautiful music.

As they left Weimar, Mitzi squeezed her brother's hand.

"We are on our way to Leipzig now," she said.

She thought of the costume safely tucked away and ready for Fritz to put on.

Mr. Toymaker was driving the horse, and Mrs. Toymaker sat beside him.

"We are on our way to Leipzig now," said Mr. Toymaker.

He thought of the famous fair to which they were going. He thought of his friend, Mr. Krauss, who would help him. But never once did he think of a concert that was to be given for him.

CHAPTER XIII

THE LEIPZIG FAIR

One of the great fairs of the year was now going on in Leipzig. The Toymakers drove by the railway station, the largest in Europe. Many people were hurrying in and out. They passed the church where Johann Sebastian Bach used to sing.

All manner of peddlers swarmed the streets. The children opened their eyes wide at sight of one man entirely covered by clocks. He was a clock peddler from the Black Forest. Traders from all over the country were in Leipzig with their wares. Buyers from every place were at the fair to buy.

"See, children," said Mrs. Toymaker. "There is a statue of Mendelssohn, the little boy who used to lead an orchestra. When he grew up, he led his orchestra in that building."

Leipzig is a city of books. Everyone seems to be reading. They read even as they stroll along the streets.

Mr. Toymaker immediately set out to find his friend, Mr. Krauss, the bookseller. But he could not find his friend.

The first day at the market place was very dismal. Nobody paid any attention to Mr. Toymaker's wares. There were too many beautiful toys to be seen.

"It is the same here as it was in Nuremberg," said Mrs. Toymaker.

Her sweet face was sad. "Oh, what are we to do?" the poor lady was thinking.

But Mitzi knew what to do. Tomorrow she and Fritz intended to slip away from their booth in the market place. Today their father needed them there to help.

Mr. Toymaker had displayed his prettiest toys: brightly colored soldiers, flaxen-haired dolls, and animals with big, staring-eyes. Yet even children did not stop. At a shop across the square were dolls that talked and walked, engines that sped along tracks, airplanes that flew, and doll houses with electric lights in them and elevators and running water. Is it any wonder that Mr. Toymaker's carved toys did not attract people?

"Run back to the wagon and make some coffee," said Mrs. Toymaker to Mitz and Fritz. "Father and I will stay here a little longer. When we get home we shall have supper."

"But there is nothing to eat in the wagon," said Mitzi.

Mrs. Toymaker looked at her husband. Mr. Toymaker turned to Mitzi.

"Obey your mother," he said. "Go home and make coffee. When we come, we shall bring food with us."

Mitz and Fritz and Frank went slowly back to the wagon.

"I do not understand how Father can bring food," said Mitzi. "There is certainly no money with which to buy it."

"Tomorrow there will be money," smiled Fritz.

"Yes," agreed Mitzi. "Because of your concert. And Father must be there to see." Suddenly she cried, "Oh, careful, you donkey! You are splashing in mud puddles. You are getting your feet all wet!"

But Fritz did not care. He was dreaming. He liked mud puddles because he was a boy. He liked dreams because he was an artist.

When they reached their wagon home, Mitzi put the coffee on the stove. Soon Mr. and Mrs. Toymaker arrived. Their arms were full of bundles.

"See what a nice supper we are to have," said Mrs. Toymaker.

She was smiling, but Mitzi noticed that there were tears in her blue eyes. Mitzi noticed something else besides the tears.

"Mother!" she cried. "Where is your pretty blue necklace?"

Mrs. Toymaker had always worn a string of sparkling blue beads. They were quite valuable and were her only piece of jewelry. She had loved them because Mr. Toymaker had given them to her before Mitz and Fritz were born.

Mrs. Toymaker did not answer Mitzi. She began to untie the bundles.

"See," she said. "Black bread and milk!"

"But, Mother," insisted Mitzi, "where is your necklace? Have you lost it?"

Mrs. Toymaker saw the terror in Mitzi's eyes. That necklace had seemed to the little girl the finest and prettiest in all the world. Her mother was not her mother without it.

Mrs. Toymaker did not know what to say. She drew Mitzi close and kissed her.

But Mr. Toymaker said, "Enough of this, Mitzi. Go and help prepare the supper. You are too curious!"

"But, Father— " began Mitzi.

"Very well, then," said Mr. Toymaker. "I shall tell you. We sold the necklace so that we could buy food. Now, are you satisfied?"

Mr. Toymaker's voice sounded cross. But his face looked very worried.

"Oh, the beautiful necklace!" cried Mitzi.

Mr. Toymaker untied a package.

"Oh, the beautiful cheese!" he sniffed.

He was trying to make the best of things. He was trying to be jolly—poor Mr. Toymaker!

"One cannot grieve about neck decorations," he said, "when the stomach cries out to be decorated!"

CHAPTER XIV

THE CONCERT

Mitzi decided to hold the concert in a park. The market square was too noisy and bustling. She wanted her brother's beautiful music to have a beautiful setting. The two children walked through Mendelssohn Street, Bach Street, Beethoven Street, and Mozart (Mō´tzärt) Street.

"Leipzig is a wonderful city," thought Fritz. "They have named their streets after their musicians."

What would Father think of that? There was no street named after a toy maker!

Bismarck Street was named for a great German leader. The strength and wisdom of Prince Otto von Bismarck helped Germany to become a powerful nation.

In the park many people strolled to and fro. Some were reading. The children came upon a silver pond with beautiful shady trees all about it.

"Now, Fritz," said Mitzi, "you must stand here beside the pond. See how peaceful it is. Your music will float across the water. It will sound like music from heaven."

Fritz put on the homemade Pied Piper cloak. Then he stood beside the pond and began to play. Several people stopped, among them a group of students with books under their arms.

"Is the young musician your brother?" asked one student of Mitzi.

"Yes," answered Mitzi. "And I am his sister."

The youths laughed and gave her a coin.

"Play some Mendelssohn, young one," they said to Fritz.

The boy obligingly played what they requested. The audience grew. Some threw coins and asked Fritz to play certain tunes. He could play nearly everything they called for. Mrs. Toymaker had been a good teacher. Besides, Fritz could play anything after he had heard it once.

Mitzi was very happy. She beamed at the crowd of listeners.

"Now," she thought, "is the time to fetch Father." She whispered to Fritz, "I am going for Father. I shall be back presently. Play until I come."

As Mitzi turned to leave, she bumped into a gentleman who carried a violin case under his arm. Mitzi did not know that this gentleman was an important music master. She hardly looked at him.

She said quickly, "Excuse me, please," and pushed her way out of the crowd. She must go for her father.

The music master stood quite still, listening. What was that he heard? What did he see? A little boy standing beside a pond, playing the violin—a little boy with a smiling face, playing the violin better than any of the music master's grown-up pupils. Who was this little boy? Where had he learned to play like that?

The music master drew closer to Fritz. He asked Fritz to play compositions by Bach and Mozart. He was astonished at how well Fritz played them.

In the meantime Mitzi hurried to her father's booth in the square.

"Father," she cried, "come! Come quickly! I have something to show you."

Mr. Toymaker jumped as if he had been shot.

"What do you mean by startling me like that?" he said to Mitzi. "You are like a young thunderbolt!"

Mitzi's cheeks were glowing. Her eyes danced.

"Fritz is playing— " she began eagerly.

But Mr. Toymaker cut her short. He was in a bad mood. He had sold no toys again today and he could not find his friend, Mr. Krauss. He was jealous, too, of the toyshop keepers who were selling their handsome wares. Now he spent his rage upon little Mitzi.

"Stop!" he cried. "Do not speak again of that boy's silly playing! Go and bring him to me now. You and he shall keep my booth for me. I am going once more to look for Mr. Krauss."

Mitzi's glowing cheeks turned pale. She pulled at her father's sleeve.

"No, no! You must come with me," she pleaded. "Please, Father, close up the booth just for a little while, until we return, and come— "

"Enough!" cried Mr. Toymaker. "Do you tell me what to do or do I tell you what to do? Now, go and fetch that lazy brother of yours. Bring him back here to help you keep my booth for me."

When poor, weeping Mitzi returned to the park, the gentleman with the violin case was still there. He stood very close to Fritz. The boy was playing a minuet. A rather large crowd still remained. Mitzi waited until Fritz finished playing the minuet. Then she went up to him.

"Oh, Fritz," she said, "Father would not come with me. He wants us to go to the market place right away."

Fritz let his violin fall to his side. A look of disappointment passed over his face and covered the smile.

"Do not leave yet," said a voice. "Play some more."

It was the music master speaking. Mitzi wiped a tear with the corner of her apron and looked at the gentleman with the violin case. His expression was kind.

"We must go," she said to him. "But we shall be back again tomorrow."

Mitzi did not know just why she said that. Only quite suddenly she had determined that she would be back tomorrow.

Some one in the crowd called, "One more selection! Come, young one; play!"

A coin came tumbling at Fritz's feet.

"Yes, yes! More music, little fiddler! More music!" cried others.

Mitzi sniffed to drive away her tears. Then she jumped upon a bench. From there she could look down upon the people. And Mitzi Toymaker began to make a speech!

"Ladies and gentlemen," she began.

Fritz thought his sister looked like a little leader. Her head was thrown back. Her two plump legs were wide apart. Her arms were folded. Fritz had to smile.

"I am glad, ladies and gentlemen," Mitzi said, "that you liked my brother's playing. Come back again tomorrow afternoon, and Fritz will give another concert!"

The people clapped their hands and shouted, "Hoch (hōk´)!" which is like "Hurrah."

Then some one called out, "What can you do, little girl?"

Mitzi gave the speaker a quick glance.

"I can do this," she said; whereupon she stood on her head.

There was a loud laugh from the crowd.

"Tomorrow, then!" cried several people.

The crowd began to move away. But the music master hesitated. Should he say something? No, he would return tomorrow. He turned his steps in the direction of home. But he could not forget the wonderful playing he had just heard. Perhaps, after hearing the little musician again tomorrow, he would try to help the youngster.

CHAPTER XV

FRITZ AND HIS VIOLIN

Sadly the brother and sister set off for the market square.

"Never mind, Fritz," said Mitzi. "We will go back to the park tomorrow. The people liked your music. They will come again, and perhaps Father will come and— "

Mitzi broke off suddenly. She stopped in the middle of the street with her mouth open.

"Fritz! Fritz!" she cried. "Oh, Fritzie!"

"What is the matter? What is it?" asked Fritz, puzzled.

He could see nothing to disturb his sister like this. He had not been walking in mud puddles.

"I have thought of the very thing!" said the girl. "I know just what we shall do. Oh, why didn't I think of it before?"

"What is it?" asked her brother.

They began to walk on again, but Mitzi was still in a state of excitement. She clutched Fritz's arm and started to talk. Her words tumbled over on top of one another, they were in such a hurry to come out.

"You shall be a real Pied Piper, Fritz!" she chattered. "Tomorrow I'll make another speech in the park. I'll ask the people to follow you just as the children followed the Pied Piper. While you are playing you will walk away. You'll be like the Piper leading the rats and the children. Only, instead of leading them to a cave, you'll lead them to— "

"Where?" asked Fritz, wide-eyed.

"To Father!" said Mitzi.

"Oh, Mitz!" cried Fritz, horrified.

"Oh, rats!" said the girl. "You'll do as I say. What fun! I know the people will follow. They are such jolly people! And what a splendid way to show Father!"

The sadness had left Mitzi. She beamed. She skipped along and sang, until Fritz caught some of her joy.

They arrived at their father's booth. But the toy maker was not there. He had closed his stand. So the children went home to their wagon. They found their father awaiting them there. The toy maker was twirling his mustache. He had a strange expression on his face.

"Now, Father," said Mitzi, "you can go and look for Mr. Krauss. Fritz and I will watch the booth for you."

But Mr. Toymaker did not move. Instead he smiled in a way which left his eyes unsmiling.

"I have decided not to go," he said. "I have decided to do something else."

"What, Father?" asked Mitzi.

"Tonight," said Mr. Toymaker, "we shall have sausage and sauerkraut and other good things for supper." Then he turned to Fritz, saying, "Give me the violin."

The boy drew away his precious violin. Mitzi stood in front of her brother.

"Father," she asked, "why do you want Fritz's violin?"

"Because I am going to sell it," said Mr. Toymaker. "It is a fine violin. It will bring much money. Besides, it is quite useless to me. Give it here."

But neither child moved. Mitz and Fritz stood like two little statues.

"Do you hear me?" cried Mr. Toymaker. "I want the violin. Give it to me."

Still they did not move. They stood looking up at the toy maker like gingerbread children out of "Hansel and Gretel."

Mr. Toymaker reached out his hand to take the violin from Fritz. But the boy put it behind his back.

"Please, please," he said, "don't take it away from me, Father!"

Now Mr. Toymaker really did not want to hurt Fritz any more than he could help. He loved this little fellow, even if he did think the boy to be only an idle, music-loving scamp.

"Fritz," he said in a kinder tone, "you will soon be a man. You must learn to bear disappointments. Come, now! Give me the violin like a good boy."

As he spoke, the toy maker took the violin from his son's hands. Then he patted Fritz on the head.

"You must learn to help others, Fritz," he said. "You must, above all, help your father."

Fritz longed to cry out and say, "But that is just what I want to do, Father!"

Only he could not speak. His eyes were full of tears, and when he brushed the tears away, the toy maker was gone. So was the boy's beloved violin!

CHAPTER XVI

THE PIED PIPER

The Toymaker family had sausage and sauerkraut and other good things for supper. They ate their supper beside a camp fire near their wagon. That is, Mr. and Mrs. Toymaker did. But Mitz and Fritz could not eat. No, even Mitz could touch nothing—not even sausage!

Mrs. Toymaker tried to comfort them, but it was hopeless. Fritz stared at the ground, and his heart ached. He thought he should never again play his violin. Mitzi sat with Frank's long nose on her lap and stroked the dog's floppy ears.

"Tomorrow," thought Mitzi, "the crowd will come to the park to hear Fritz play, and there will be no Fritz!"

Of course, Mitzi did not know that the music master would come, too. The kind music master would return. He would look for the little boy whose music had pleased him so much. He would wonder what had happened to the clever youngster whom he wanted to help. Mitzi did not know this. If she had known it, she would have been more unhappy than she already was.

The next morning passed much the same as the day before. Mr. Toymaker sold nothing at his booth in the market place.

At noon he said, "There is no use staying here any longer."

He closed up his booth, and they went back to the wagon. After lunch Mr. and Mrs. Toymaker sat upon the steps of their wagon. They talked and talked about what they were to do.

"We could go to some small town and settle down," said Mrs. Toymaker. "When winter comes, a wandering life will not be very pleasant. Mitz and Fritz should go to school. This gypsy life is not the best life for them."

Mr. Toymaker said, "That is quite true. Let us find a town where people are not spoiled by fine toys. There we shall settle and be content to live simply."

"I do wish—" began Mrs. Toymaker.

She had started to talk about Fritz. However, she knew that it made Mr. Toymaker angry. So she stopped.

They sat together for a long time. Mrs. Toymaker knitted. Mr. Toymaker smoked a pipe. Both were so full of serious thoughts that they did not wonder about Mitz and Fritz. They did not wonder why the children had not been there since noon. As the shadows grew longer and a little late breeze blew up, Mrs. Toymaker arose.

"I must prepare supper," she said. "I wonder where the children are."

She called, "Fritz! Mitz!" But there was no answer.

"What is that I see in the distance?" asked Mr. Toymaker.

He shaded his eyes with his hand. He looked in the direction of the setting sun. Mrs. Toymaker looked, too. Black forms were coming toward them. A crowd of people was drawing near, following some one who made music.

"Listen," said Mrs. Toymaker. "The notes of a violin!"

Mr. Toymaker stood up. The music, sweet and lively, came to them more clearly. Slowly the forms of the people grew more distinct as they drew closer.

"Why, it is a Pied Piper!" exclaimed Mrs. Toymaker. "It must be the joke of some children."

But all the time Mrs. Toymaker thought she knew who it was. She thought she knew that it was really—Yes, now there could be no doubt about it!

"It is Fritz!" cried Mrs. Toymaker. "It is our own little Fritz!"

CHAPTER XVII

THE MUSIC MASTER

The strange procession stopped before the wagon of the toy maker. The Pied Piper continued his playing. The crowd stood listening. When the piece was finished, they clapped and threw coins and shouted, "Hoch!"

Then a gentleman carrying a violin case hoisted the Pied Piper upon his shoulder. He walked over with the Pied Piper to where the toy maker stood.

"Sir," said the violin-case gentleman, "I believe this is your son."

Mr. Toymaker was so amazed that he could only nod his head.

The gentleman went on, "Your son's playing has made us all very happy. We followed his music just as the children of long ago followed the Pied Piper of Hamelin."

The people began to laugh and cheer and call for more music.

But Mr. Violin-Case said, "The concert is over. Now I am going to see Mr. Toymaker alone."

When the people had left, Mr. Violin-Case and Mr. Toymaker went into the wagon together. There they stayed for quite a long time.

Outside, Mrs. Toymaker drew her children close to her.

"Tell me," she said. "Do tell me all about it."

Mitzi said, "Good! I'll tell you, Mother. But first I must have a pretzel to eat. I have had nothing since morning."

Mitzi helped herself to a fistful of the salty, twisted crackers. She began to eat and to talk at the same time—a feat which cannot be done very well.

Her words sounded to Mrs. Toymaker like "Yummeemummee."

The mother laughed and said, "Fritz had better tell me."

Fritz began, "Mitzi believed all along that people would really like my music. She wanted to show Father. So today we went back to the same park where I played yesterday."

By this time, Mitzi had swallowed her first pretzel, so she continued the story: "I stood upon a bench. I talked very loudly so everyone could hear. I said that our father had sold Fritz's violin and that Fritz could not play for them. I said I was sorry that we could not keep our promise and give another concert. Then the gennamemmaeppa – "

"Mitzi!" laughed Mrs. Toymaker. "How can I understand you when you are eating pretzels?"

"The gentleman stepped up to us," went on Fritz.

"What gentlemen, dear?"

"The one who is in the wagon with Father," said Fritz.

"He has a red face, and he stands like this," said Mitzi.

She stuck out her stomach trying to imitate the gentleman who was rather large.

"Shame, Mitzi!" said her mother. "Go on, please, Fritz. Tell me the rest."

"The gentleman said he would help us," Fritz continued. "He took this beautiful violin out of its case and gave it to me." Tenderly Fritz laid the violin in his mother's hands. "He told me to play it. I did, and he seemed to like what I played."

"After the concert," interrupted Mitzi, "I jumped up on the bench again. I asked the people to follow Fritz just as if he were the Pied Piper."

"At first," broke in Fritz, "they laughed and didn't want to. But the gentleman urged them to do it. He said it would be fun. He said he would like to see where I would lead them."

"And this is where we led them," said Mitzi.

"Now," said Fritz, "Father will know that what we told him is true."

Mrs. Toymaker looked very happy. She hugged Fritz to her. Just then Mr. Toymaker came out of the wagon with the violin-case gentleman.

"This is Mr. Schmitt," said the toy maker to his family. "Mr. Schmitt is a great music master from Berlin."

Fritz's eyes began to pop. Mitzi sat down with a jolt, her mouth open. Mrs. Toymaker felt her heart beating very fast.

The music master went up to Fritz and took his hand.

"I have just had a talk with your father, Fritz," he said. "You are coming with me to Berlin. You are all coming to live in the big city of Berlin. And you, Fritz, will study and in time will become a great musician."

Mr. Schmitt stayed to supper with the family. He sat with them beside their gypsy fire. He told them about Berlin and promised to help Mr. Toymaker because of Fritz's music.

He said to the toy maker, "Your little boy has a gift from God. You must help him make it a gift to the world."

As they sat about the fire after supper Mr. Schmitt told them about another boy.

"Many years ago," he said, "there lived a boy named George Handel (Hăn´del). He was born in Halle (Häl´ẽ), a town not far from here. Today there is a statue of George Handel in the center of Halle. He became a famous composer. But when he was your age, Fritz, his father would not allow him to play."

Fritz looked at his mother. Mitzi looked at her father. The toy maker looked away from them all.

"You see," went on Mr. Schmitt, "George's father was a good man. But he did not love music. He wanted his son to be a doctor. Now, one day little George played for a powerful duke, who loved music. The duke decided to help young George.

"He said to Mr. Handel, 'You are a good man. But your son will be a great man. His music will fill people's hearts with beauty. Can you do that?'"

CHAPTER XVIII

BERLIN AND HAPPINESS

The Toymakers and Mr. Schmitt flew to Berlin in an airplane. People in Germany travel by plane as easily as we travel by train and boat. Berlin is the capital of Germany. The Berlin airport is the largest in the world.

As the children stepped out of the plane they heard music. They saw people sitting about at tables eating and drinking. These people were watching the landings of the different airships.

"Come. We shall go to my home," said Mr. Schmitt. "I have a large house near the music school. I want you to stay there with me until you find a home of your own."

They drove in a taxicab through the Brandenburg Gate and into a famous street, Unter den Linden (Ōōn´tĕr dĕn Lĭn´dĕn). New York has Fifth Avenue. London has Piccadilly Circus. Chicago has Lake Shore Drive. Edinburgh has Princes Street. And Berlin has Unter den Linden.

They drove along the wide, shady boulevard with its flower beds, lawns, and fountains. What a splendid street!

The children's joy and excitement made them unusually quiet. It was very wonderful to be riding through this fine city and to know that their struggles and hardships were over.

Mr. Toymaker had sold his wagon. Mr. Schmitt planned to find him work in a big Berlin toy shop. Later, the kind music master intended to find a cosy home for the family. Mitz and Fritz were going to school. Fritz would study music and practice on his violin. One day he would be able to give real concerts.

Mr. Schmitt lived in an old-fashioned house, which seemed beautiful to the children. It was full of ornaments and heavy furniture. Great pictures of musicians hung upon the walls.

Mitz, Fritz, and their dog immediately explored the house from attic to cellar. In the kitchen, Mitzi found a jolly cook, who gave her cookies. Yes, Mitzi knew that she was going to like Berlin!

Fritz found musical instruments in every room. Sounds of piano and violin and flute came from all quarters of the house. No, never before in all his life had Fritz been so happy!

That evening, when the children were in bed, Mr. and Mrs. Toymaker sat talking.

"It is true," said Mr. Toymaker to his wife. "You were right. Fritz has turned beauty into gold. People will pay for things even if they cannot touch them."

Mrs. Toymaker replied, "But even if they cannot touch music, music can touch them."

At last Mr. Toymaker agreed.

"It can touch their hearts," he said.